Puffin Books

Arthur and the Great Detective

Heading for England aboard the storm-tossed
S.S. *Murgatroyd*, the amazing schoolboy detective, Arthur William Foskett, encounters Sherlock
Holmes and Dr Watson. This epic meeting of
super-sleuths results in their putting their wits
together to solve the Mystery of the Missing
Manuscript.

In their investigations they meet the strangest
bunch of suspects ever to board a ship, Gilbert and
Sullivan, the half-crazed Duchess of Cricklewood,
the curious Tattooed Steward, Scarlet 'Orace and
a Singing Lifeboat!

Follow the exploits of these intrepid detectives
as they unravel one of the most puzzling crimes of
the century.

Arthur and Sherlock Holmes solve more baffl-
ing mysteries in *Arthur and the Bellybutton
Diamond*, which is also available in Puffin.

ALAN COREN

ARTHUR
AND THE GREAT
DETECTIVE

Illustrated by John Astrop

PUFFIN BOOKS

Puffin Books, Penguin Books Ltd, Harmondsworth, Middlesex, England
Penguin Books, 625 Madison Avenue, New York, New York 10022, U.S.A.
Penguin Books Australia Ltd, Ringwood, Victoria, Australia
Penguin Books Canada Ltd, 2801 John Street, Markham, Ontario, Canada L3R 1B4
Penguin Books (N.Z.) Ltd, 182–190 Wairau Road, Auckland 10, New Zealand

First published by Robson Books 1979

Published in Puffin Books 1981

Made and printed in Great Britain by
Richard Clay (The Chaucer Press) Ltd,
Bungay, Suffolk
Set in Monophoto Times

For Harriet and Ned

Once upon a time, about a hundred years ago, in the very middle of the black and wintry Atlantic Ocean, rolled a ship.

It did not only roll. It pitched; it heaved; it lurched. Sometimes, it trembled from bow to stern with a terrible grinding shudder, as a particularly enormous storm-blown wave carried it so high that its propellers cleared the dark water and threshed in empty air for several seconds; and after that, it would tremble from stern to bow as it crashed down again into a swirling foam-white trough, the icy waters smashing across its decks and hissing back out through the rails and rigging as the terrible sea swept the ship upwards once more.

Naturally enough, the passengers aboard the S.S. *Murgatroyd* were far from happy. They had all of them bought their tickets on a fine crisp October morning in New York, with the sun winking on a calm blue Atlantic, gulls honking cheerily in the cloudless sky, a uniformed band playing bright brassy marching songs on the pier as the ship made ready to sail for England, and everything, in short, looking set fair for a smooth trip east. With three thousand miles to sail and two weeks to sail them in, the passengers – as the sirens blew on the two tall funnels, and the four fat little tugs began to pull the S.S. *Murgatroyd* slowly away from the pier – looked forward to long leisurely days of fresh sea breezes and jolly deck games, and long leisurely nights of lying in snug bunks and gazing through their portholes at the brilliant stars until the gentle rocking of the big ship lulled them into deep and peaceful sleep.

It did not turn out that way at all.

On the morning of the second day, as the passengers, smartly dressed in their fashionable travelling clothes, took their stroll around the spotless deck, the gentlemen doffing their stove-pipe hats at the ladies, and the ladies smiling politely beneath their new pink parasols at the elegant gentlemen, and nobody thinking of anything more important than whether there would be chocolate biscuits with their morning cocoa or whether there would be plum cake, something very ominous happened.

Two small white clouds which had been floating along separately in the sunny sky suddenly joined together to make a somewhat larger white cloud. Which began to grow. And after perhaps half an hour, there was more cloud than sky, and after another half an hour, there was no sky at all, and the ceiling of cloud had turned grey. Worse, a wind had come up, and one or two pink parasols had been whipped from the ladies' hands and these had whirled overboard, to bob in the white wake, and slightly puzzle the fish.

By the time the cocoa arrived at eleven o'clock, quite a few of the passengers had stopped caring whether they were going to get chocolate biscuits or plum cake; the new and unfamiliar movement of the S.S. *Murgatroyd* seemed to have had a strange effect on their appetites. They stared at their cocoa somewhat gloomily; and their gloom deepened even further when the surface of the cocoa began to go plop. Within seconds, the noise of rain drumming on stove-pipe hats had become surprisingly loud, and within very few more seconds, a number of parasols (which had been intended only to keep the sun off) began to shrink; and within even fewer seconds after that, the raindrops were pelting down like bullets!

And by the time three more days had passed, with the storm still raging, the passengers were split into two clear categories: those who moaned and went white, or those who groaned and went green.

All the passengers, that is, but three.

Every morning, in the elegant panelled dining-room of the S.S. *Murgatroyd*, thirty tables were laid for breakfast; every noon, thirty were laid for lunch; and every evening, thirty were laid for dinner. Each table was set for four people. But every day, only two of these tables were occupied, and neither of those was occupied by four. One table on the port side was always occupied by two smartly dressed gentlemen; and one table on the starboard side was always occupied by a small boy. (You may perhaps be wondering why there was no Captain's table, since you have probably heard that steamships traditionally have a table where the Captain entertains important guests. And indeed, the S.S. *Murgatroyd* would have had one if the weather hadn't been quite so dreadful; as it was, the Captain never left the bridge, preferring to stay at his post to keep an eye on things and living on his favourite food, small oblongs of fried minced cod, a dish which had been invented by his sister, Mrs Alice Fishfinger.)

The two gentlemen were an interesting-looking pair. One was very tall, and very bony, with a sharp triangular nose that somehow, and curiously, suggested that he was remarkably clever. His plaid Inverness cape and his plaid deerstalker hat were always laid across one of the other chairs

10

at his table, as if in constant readiness should he suddenly wish to dash from the room. Which, in fact, he occasionally did. His companion was shorter and stouter, and given to eating enormous quantities of food and drinking enormous quantities of wine, after which he would very carefully wipe his mouth on his napkin, take a stethoscope from the pocket of his black tailcoat, and listen to his heart.

Nor was the small boy on the other side of the dining-room any less interesting than the two men. He appeared to be travelling alone, which itself was quite remarkable on a transatlantic passage, ate everything that was put in front of him, including squid, tapioca, and quite fatty lamb chops, never played with his cutlery, and, above all, seemed to be totally without fear. Once, indeed, when the ship gave a particularly terrible lurch during the soup course and the Chief Steward dropped his tureen and screamed, despite being a huge bearded man with tattooed hands like bunches of hairy bananas, the small boy actually told him, quietly, politely, yet very firmly, to pull himself together and set an example to the rest of the crew; and after that, the Chief Steward never screamed again, nor dropped anything at all.

The other stewards, however, gradually disappeared one by one as the crossing grew worse; until, on the ninth day, which is when our story really begins, the Chief Steward, having first spoken at lunch to the two gentlemen, then lurched across to address the small boy.

'Excuse me,' he said, 'but I wonder if you'd very much mind joining the gentlemen at the other table? The thing is, all the other stewards are feeling a bit off colour, and as I'm the only person serving, it would help me very much if all three of you sat at the same table.'

'Of course not,' said the small boy, who was very considerate.

And he got up, and walked across the dining-room very steadily, and sat down between the stout black gentleman and the chair with the Inverness cape on it.

'Good day,' he said, 'my name is Arthur.'

'How d'you do?' said the stout man cheerily. 'My name is Doctor Watson, and this is Mr Sherlock Holmes.'

'How do you do?' replied Arthur. He glanced at Doctor Watson. 'You have been in Afghanistan, I see.'

'How on earth do you know that?' he cried.

Arthur cleared his throat. Not noisily, of course.

'I hope you won't think I'm rude,' he said, 'but I couldn't help thinking: Here is a gentleman of a medical type, but with the air of a military man. Clearly, an army doctor, then. He has just come from the tropics, for his face is dark, and that's not the natural colour of his skin, because his wrists are pale. He has been ill, because his face is haggard, and his left arm has been injured, because he holds it in a stiff and unnatural manner. Where in the tropics could an English army doctor have gone through a bad time and got his arm wounded? Clearly, because there's a war on there, nowhere but Afghanistan.'

'I say!' cried Watson. 'That's dashed clever!'

'On the contrary,' said Arthur modestly, 'it's elementary.'

Sherlock Holmes, who had been listening intently, now murmured:

'What an extraordinary boy!'

'Thank you,' said Arthur. 'Of course, he hasn't *just* come from Afghanistan, because he's been in America with you doing some detective work.'

'Goodness me!' exclaimed Sherlock Holmes. 'How in heaven's name did you know I was a detective?'

'Well,' said Arthur, 'I noticed that huge magnifying glass you have in your top pocket, which you don't use for looking at the menu, so I knew it wasn't for reading. Also, you never walk on deck without your stick, but you're a very fit man who walks very fast and you obviously don't need it to help you walk, because most of the time you just carry it, so I thought to myself: that must be a swordstick.'

'It is, it is!' cried Watson. 'And made by Wibley and Grindell, perhaps the finest makers of –'

But here Holmes, who was looking at Arthur

very keenly indeed, restrained Doctor Watson with a finger to his lips.

'*And*,' continued Arthur, 'when we came on board, I noticed two things: first, you had no trunk, only a small bag, and second, a very important-looking American policeman shook your hand as you started up the gangplank. So I have been considering what sort of Englishman goes to America for a very short stay, carries a magnifying glass and a swordstick, and is well known to the New York police, and there was only one –'

'Conclusion,' finished Sherlock Holmes, nodding. 'Yes, Arthur, there usually is. You concluded that I had been to America on a detective mission, and you were absolutely right. That, however, no longer surprises me. For I, in my turn,

15

have deduced that you must be none other than Arthur William Foskett!'

'Amazing!' shouted Watson.

'Elementary,' murmured Sherlock Holmes. 'Isn't it, Arthur?'

'Well –' said Arthur, modestly.

'This boy,' said Holmes to his baffled friend, 'has been variously known, in his short yet remarkable career, as Buffalo Arthur, The Lone Arthur, Arthur the Kid, Railroad Arthur, Klondike Arthur –'

'Aliases?' cried Doctor Watson in horror. 'You mean he is some kind of criminal, Holmes? How absolutely appalling, he cannot be more than eight or nine, and his table manners are beyond reproach, who would have thought that underneath it all he is nothing but a dastardly and villainous –'

'Oh, do shut up, Watson,' said Holmes, wearily. 'Arthur here is a hero, and a lawful one at that.'

Arthur blushed deeply.

'Not to mention,' went on Sherlock Holmes, 'a considerable detective who has foiled bank robbers, train robbers, cattle rustlers *and* pirates! He is famous. It is even said that books are being written about him.'

'Good heavens!' exclaimed Watson. 'What a good idea! Perhaps I should write one about *you*, Holmes!'

The great detective looked at him sharply.

'Don't be silly, Watson!' he snapped. 'You know my methods.'

'Well?'

'Would I want every criminal in England to know them, too?' asked Holmes.

'What a pity,' sighed Watson. 'This American case would have made a marvellous tale, Holmes.'

'I do not give a fig,' and here Sherlock Holmes snapped his long bony fingers, 'for marvellous tales, as you call them! My object is the solution of crime and the apprehension of the criminal. But tell me, Arthur,' he went on, turning to the small boy, 'why are you going to England?'

'I would call it,' murmured Watson, '*A Study in Scarlet.*'

Sherlock Holmes put down his fork. He looked at Doctor Watson, and his eyes glittered like knife blades caught in firelight. If that's how he looks at his *friends*, thought Arthur, I certainly shouldn't like to be one of his enemies.

'Sorry, Holmes,' mumbled Watson. 'Would you care for a sprout?'

'NO!'

'I'm going to England,' said Arthur quickly, recognizing that even though it was rude to interrupt, it was probably better than letting the two of them go on like this, 'because I'm returning to school. I only spend my holidays in America.'

'Aha!' cried Sherlock Holmes, thumping the table with such force that the pepperpots jumped

17

like mice. '*That* explains why we have never heard of any English exploits of yours! You only carry them out in your holidays.'

Arthur nodded.

'You know how boring holidays can get,' he said.

'Quite,' agreed Holmes vigorously.

'Oh, I don't know,' said Doctor Watson, swallowing a potato whole and washing it down with a huge glug of wine, 'I rather like holidays. You can get a lot of eating done.'

Sherlock Holmes pushed back his chair, and stood up.

'Watson, my old friend, would you excuse me if I took a turn around the deck? Since I have finished my luncheon, I rather thought I might smoke a –'

'Finished your luncheon?' exclaimed Watson. 'Why Holmes, according to the menu there are three different pies to come, not to mention a wide selection of fruit jellies, sherry trifle, and an extremely interesting thing I saw on the trolley which seems absolutely crammed with walnuts, to say nothing of a cherry on the top! *And* there's cheese.'

'I leave you to it,' cried Holmes cheerily, snatching up his cape and hat, and gripping his sword-stick firmly. 'You and Arthur may draw lots for the cherry.'

'No, thank you,' said Arthur, putting his knife and fork together, 'I've had enough.'

.Watson stared at him. He shook his head.

'Boys today,' he murmured. 'What is happening? Where will it end?'

'In that case,' said Sherlock Holmes to Arthur, 'perhaps you would care to accompany me?'

'Oh, yes, please!' said Arthur, and together they went out of the dining-room, leaving the good doctor waving eagerly at the tattooed steward.

'It isn't that he's greedy, you know,' said Holmes, as they stood on deck.

'Of course not,' replied Arthur. 'It's just that he didn't get much jelly or cheese in Afghanistan, isn't it?'

'Exactly,' said Sherlock Holmes. He took an enormous yellow pipe from his pocket, and began stuffing it with great chunks of black tobacco.

'That's an interesting smell,' said Arthur, after Sherlock Holmes had lit up and was puffing huge greeny-blue gusts of smoke from his two long nostrils (and looking a bit like the S.S. *Murgatroyd* herself, thought Arthur, except her funnels aren't upside down; though, of course, he didn't say so).

'Yes,' said Holmes, 'it is a tobacco I designed myself, Arthur, made up of equal parts of Old Black Pongy and Thick Dark Gunge, with a pinch of Parson Nasty's Ancient Turkish Mixture. There are one hundred and eighty-seven different sorts of tobacco, you know. I have,' and here Sherlock Holmes puffed out his bony chest just a little, 'written a paper on the subject.'

'How interesting,' said Arthur politely.

'Yes,' replied Sherlock Holmes, 'it can often help in the deduction of crime.'

'I know,' said Arthur. 'I've written a paper on different sorts of toffee, for the same reason.'

'Really?' said Sherlock Holmes. 'Are there many different sorts of toffee?'

'Three hundred and nine,' said Arthur.

Sherlock Holmes blinked. His great pipe seemed to sag a little, and some of the puff appeared to have gone out of his chest.

'Oh,' he murmured.

'It looks as though the storm's dying out,' said Arthur, suddenly feeling that he ought to change the subject, and they both looked up to where one or two patches of blue were showing through the breaking cloud.

'The wind is dropping, too,' said Sherlock Holmes, and as he remarked upon it, the roar of the gale, over which they had been shouting, suddenly fell away altogether.

And they could hear someone singing.

'Curious,' commented Holmes.

'I thought everyone was ill,' said Arthur. 'Unless, of course, it's Doctor Watson who's singing.'

The great detective shook his head firmly.

'Never! If Watson goes to the trouble of opening his mouth wide enough to sing, you may be sure it's only because he wants to put food inside it.' Holmes peered around the deck. 'Most strange, Arthur. There is no one in sight.'

They listened again, cupping their ears. The voice, a deep, male, and rather melodious one, sang on.

'It seems,' said Arthur, 'to be coming from that lifeboat.'

They tiptoed across – no easy thing on a wet and

rolling deck – and put their ears to the side of the canvas-covered boat.

And they heard:

'When I first put this uniform on,
I said as I looked in the glass:
It's one to a million that any civilian
My figure and form could surpass.'

Holmes glanced keenly down the white length of the lifeboat at Arthur.

'A stowaway!' he hissed. And, taking a firm grip

on his stick with one hand and a firm grip on the edge of the canvas with the other, he whipped off the cover!

There, crouched amidships, sat no stowaway but the ship's Bosun! He looked startled; but, then, who wouldn't be?

'Yes?' he said, when he'd got his breath back.

'I'm sorry, Bosun,' said Sherlock Holmes, 'my friend Arthur and I heard noises, and we assumed that, well –'

'I like to come in here sometimes for a bit of a lie down,' said the Bosun. 'I can take my leg off without making people feel uncomfortable.'

It was true! Beside the Bosun lay his shiny wooden leg, unstrapped.

Well, you can just imagine how embarrassed Holmes and Arthur both felt.

'I do most humbly apologize,' murmured Sherlock Holmes.

'We had no idea,' said Arthur.

'That's all right,' said the Bosun, grinning. 'The thing with a wooden leg is, you get a bit of an itch from time to time. So it's nice to whip it off and have a bit of a scratch. 'Course, it's not the sort of thing you want to do in public.'

'Absolutely,' mumbled Holmes. 'Quite understand, old chap.'

The Bosun eased himself up, glanced around, sniffed the air with his great red nose.

'Hum! Weather's cheering up, I see,' he said.

'Have to be getting back to work. The passengers'll be up and about any time now. Mind turning your backs, gents, while I strap on Old Percy?'

Well, as you can probably guess, the two detectives did more than just turn their backs! After such an awkward moment, they needed no second opportunity to get away from that lifeboat as fast as their legs would carry them. Indeed, so fast were they hurrying that, as they turned a corner on the afterdeck, they almost bowled over a tall man with a bright red beard who was just emerging from the saloon.

Holmes stepped back.

'Excuse me,' he apologized.

'My fault entirely,' said the bearded man.

And politely raised his hat, before hurrying on.

Holmes, who had in his turn raised his deerstalker, began to walk on with Arthur, when he suddenly stopped.

'Good heavens!' he cried. 'Curse me for a fool! I was still so shaken by the curious incident of the Bosun's leg that my observation was a thousand miles away! Did you notice anything odd about that man we just bumped into?'

'As a matter of fact,' replied Arthur, 'I did. I didn't say anything, because it is extremely rude to make personal remarks, but although his beard was red, when he raised his hat to us, his hair was –'

'Exactly!' shouted Holmes. 'His hair was jet black!'

He spun around, but the man had gone.

'Now why,' said Sherlock Holmes, 'should a perfectly respectable passenger be wearing a false beard? The only conclusion we may arrive at, Arthur, is that he was not a perfectly respectable passenger at all! He has either recently committed some fearful crime, or is just about to. Quick, we must find him!'

'Wait a moment, Mr Holmes,' cried Arthur, 'suppose it was the –'

But it was too late. Whatever Arthur had intended to point out to the great detective remained unpointed, for Sherlock Holmes had sprinted off down the deck in pursuit of the red-bearded man. The few passengers who, the sea having calmed, had begun to emerge a little unsteadily from their cabins now flattened themselves against the walls of the deckhouse to avoid being run down by the swooping figure of Holmes, zigzagging through them, cape-flaps flying, for all the world like a giant bat.

Arthur followed as quickly as he could, and caught up with Holmes as he stopped for a moment in the shadow of the forward funnel, trying to decide which way to turn.

'Vanished!' snapped Holmes. 'We are dealing with a –'

'AAARGH! Take that, you villain!'

The cry had come from the other side of the ship. It was followed immediately by a terrible crash and the sound of splintering glass, at which two lady passengers, who had just come out on deck after seven wretched days below, fainted on the spot, and at least three gentlemen decided to write letters to the steamship company in the strongest possible terms, almost certainly asking for their money back.

Holmes, however, had more than that on *his* mind.

'Great gumboils, Arthur!' he shouted. 'That was

Doctor Watson's voice. He must have grappled with the rogue!'

Within seconds, they had burst into the dining-room, and there indeed was the trusty doctor, rolling on the ground with his adversary in a great whirling flurry of arms and legs, the two of them blurring into what the casual eye might have taken to be an octopus gone mad!

'Hold him, Watson!' roared Holmes.

'Wurrrgh! Ouch! I've got him, Holmes!' bellowed Watson.

And so he had.

But after Sherlock Holmes had flung himself upon the two of them and dragged them apart, Arthur noticed that it was not the tall, red-bearded man at all, but a small wiry person with a black moustache, the rest of his face being invisible

beneath his pork-pie hat which had been jammed down over his eyes and nose during the fierce struggle.

'Good Lord, Watson,' cried Holmes, 'but this is not our fellow at all!'

'*Your* fellow?' inquired Watson, recovering his breath and rapidly putting his stethoscope to his chest to make sure nothing had gone wrong inside. 'What do you mean, *your* fellow? That man is *my* fellow, if he's anybody's. Two minutes ago, he strode in here, big as you please, announced that now the storm was over he'd got his appetite back, and attempted to take from the pudding trolley the big piece of lovely walnut thing which I had expressly ordered for myself. In short, Holmes' – and here Doctor Watson's face grew most un-usually severe, as he glared at the man wriggling in his friend's grasp – 'the piece with the cherry on it!'

Sherlock Holmes stared at Watson. The terrible glitter had come back into his eyes. Arthur suddenly felt very nervous.

'Is – that – all – Watson?' hissed Holmes, through gritted teeth.

'It's quite enough!' snapped the doctor. 'It's not as if cherries grow on trees. At least,' he added quickly, 'in the middle of the Atlantic they don't.'

Arthur shut his eyes, and held his breath, and waited for Sherlock Holmes to do something terrible to his podgy friend; but by the greatest good luck, at that moment the little man inside the jammed hat chose to shout:

'OY! Wot about someone pullin' my 'at orf?'

And since Holmes was the nearest, he instantly put good manners before personal feelings and, standing on the little man's feet to give himself some leverage, he tugged off the pork-pie hat.

And immediately gasped aloud!

'Why, it's Inspector Lestrade!'

Watson went white.

'Of Scotland Yard?' he muttered. 'Oh Lord!'

'Quite!' snapped the little policeman. 'Absolutely! That is to say, not 'alf!' He glowered at Watson. He took out an enormous black notebook. He licked a stubby pencil, flicking his tongue (thought Watson miserably) like a snake. 'I am arresting you,' barked Lestrade, 'on nine charges. First, jumping on people. Second, ruining people's 'ats. Third, rippin' orf people's buttons. Fourth, grievously and with malice aforethought snatching people's cherries out from under their very –'

Sherlock Holmes put up his hand.

'Just a moment, Inspector,' he said. 'I am afraid you can't arrest people here, you know. The S.S. *Murgatroyd* is a ship, and the only person allowed to make arrests on board ship is the Captain.'

'Good thinking!' muttered Watson to Arthur.

'Elementary,' murmured Arthur.

Lestrade shrugged, and put his notebook away.

'Worth a try, anyhow,' he said.

'That is as maybe,' replied Holmes irritably. 'While we've been wasting time here, a somewhat more desperate criminal than Doctor Watson has had the chance to get clean away.'

'Criminal?' repeated Lestrade. 'What kind of criminal?'

'A tall and sinister fellow,' replied Holmes, 'with a bright red beard.'

'Scarlet 'Orace!' cried Lestrade.

'Scarlet Horace?' said Holmes. 'You know the man, then?'

The little policeman tutted impatiently.

'No, no, no! The Scarlet 'Orace is the priceless ruby belonging to the Duchess of Cricklewood, named after the man wot give it 'er, 'er ninth 'usband, the millionaire tobacconist Sir 'Orace Whiff.'

'I fail to see the connection,' muttered Sherlock Holmes, 'between this gem and our bearded friend.'

'I am 'ere on this boat,' explained Lestrade,

mopping his brow with a plain-clothes handker-chief, 'to guard the Scarlet 'Orace. I accompanied the Duchess to America with it last week, on account of she was going to wear it to the first night of a hopera entitled *The Pirates of Penzance* in New York. So we all came over on the boat, and we all went to the aforementioned hopera to-gether, and now we are all going back 'ome again. At least,' he added grimly, 'I bloomin' well 'ope we are!'

'Quite,' nodded Holmes. 'With this red-bearded criminal aboard, and I have no doubt that it is the Scarlet Horace he is after, who can say what might – tell me, Inspector, where is the ruby now?'

'Werl,' replied Lestrade, 'it *ought* to be round 'er Grace's neck.'

'Where's that?' inquired Watson.

The Inspector glared at him scornfully.

'I'd 'ave thought you'd 'ave known that,' he said, 'being a medical man. It's between 'er Grace's body and 'er Grace's 'ead, of course. Calls himself a doctor!'

'No, no, *no*!' snapped Holmes. 'What he means is where is 'er Grace, I mean *Her* Grace, now?'

'Cabin next to mine,' replied Lestrade. 'Unless a certain red-bearded individual 'as got there first.'

Whereupon they all rushed out.

All, that is, except Arthur.

*

For Arthur had his doubts.

He walked thoughtfully from the dining-room into the forward saloon, and he sat down in a deep brown leather armchair for a bit of a rest. It had, after all, been a somewhat hectic afternoon.

'Glad the weather's perked up a little,' said a voice.

Arthur looked round. In the chair next to his, but so sunk down in it that he had not at first noticed him, was a gentleman of perhaps forty, in extravagant mutton-chop side-whiskers and a rather garish rainbow-silk waistcoat. He was picking his large white teeth with a tuning fork.

'So am I,' answered Arthur. 'Are you a musician, by any chance?'

'Of course,' said the gentleman. 'And not by chance, either,' he went on, rather sternly. 'I am a musician by hard work, by concentration, by enterprise, and, it goes without saying, by genius.'

Well, thought Arthur, it hadn't *actually* gone without saying. But, of course, he did not point this out.

The gentleman then struck the tuning fork against his forehead, held it to his ear, and was quietly beaming to himself and humming in tune when a sudden sharp yell wiped the beam from his lip and the hum from his throat.

'ARTHUR! ARE YOU IN HERE?'

'Oh, bother!' muttered the musician, curling himself into a ball and giving every impression that he was trying to corkscrew himself into his chair. 'Don't give me away! Don't tell him I'm here.'

'But it's me he's after,' whispered Arthur back to him, 'whoever he is. *I'm* Arthur.'

The musician started to protest, but thought better of it. He put a finger to his lips. They heard feet scurry past outside, and the voice shouting 'ARTHUR!' growing fainter as its owner hurried away along the open deck.

'Phew!' phewed the musician, and sat up. 'That was close. Now, what's all this nonsense about your being Arthur?'

'It isn't nonsense at all. I am Arthur William Foskett.'

'What a coincidence!' exclaimed the musician. 'I am Arthur Seymour Sullivan.'

Arthur's (that's to say Arthur William Foskett's) mouth dropped open.

'Are you really?' he cried. 'Then *he* must be –'

'William Schwenck Gilbert,' said Sullivan. 'Yes, he is. We are Gilbert and Sullivan. Or, as I prefer to think of it, Sullivan and Gilbert.'

'I saw *H.M.S.Pinafore* last year,' said Arthur. 'I thought it was marvellous. And I'm going to see *The Pirates of Penzance* when I get back to London. Inspector Lestrade was just talking about it, he said you opened it in New York.'

'Yes,' said Sullivan. 'That's where we've been. Going back home now, got to start getting our latest one together; after we've opened *Pirates* in London, of course.'

'What's the new one called?'

'*Patience*,' replied Sullivan. 'Going to have some wonderful tunes.' He sniffed. 'Shouldn't think Gilbert's words'll be up to much, though. They never are. Lot of rubbish; just get in the way of the music, if you want my opinion.'

'SO THERE YOU ARE!'

A small plump man in a nightshirt had suddenly appeared in front of them, as if spirited there by some weird conjuring trick! One foot was slippered, the other bare, and pink with cold: his five fat toes looked like boiled prawns. He quivered all over, from his podgy pink foot to his podgy purple

face, and he breathed through his nostrils in little snorts. He shook his fist in Sullivan's startled face.

'Gilbert,' said Sullivan sharply, 'go and get your trousers on. Can't you see we have company?'

'*Company?*' shrieked W. S. Gilbert, his eyes rolling about like marbles in a saucer. '*Trousers?* We stand here ruined, and all you can think of is etiquette!'

Sullivan sighed elegantly, and smiled a small weary smile at Arthur.

'I'm afraid I must beg you to forgive Gilbert,' he said. 'He does tend to go on a bit. It comes of believing himself to be a poet. Goodness knows why a tiny talent like being able to rhyme cat with mat should make certain people feel they have the right to go potty in public, but there you are.' He glared at his agitated colleague, and a hard edge came into his voice. 'Gilbert sometimes seems to forget, my dear Arthur, that he and I are no longer struggling artists, but Important Figures in International Society! WE DO NOT,' and his own voice had risen, now, to a furious shriek, 'GO AROUND WITHOUT SOCKS!'

Gilbert suddenly went flat, like a burst balloon. He sat down on the carpet.

'*Patience*,' he groaned, 'is gone.'

'Mine certainly is,' snapped Sullivan. 'Why can't you sit in a chair like a normal human being?'

'*Patience*,' said Gilbert, 'our next opera. Your music. My wonderful words. Our only copy of the manuscript. Gone! Vanished! Pouf!'

Sullivan sprang to his feet.

'You don't mean, you can't be saying, it isn't possible, it couldn't happen!' he spluttered.

Gilbert shook his head.

'Oh, I do; I am; it is,' he moaned, 'and it did!'

Sullivan dropped to his knees beside his friend, as Arthur watched, miserable for them both.

'But it was all locked up in the tin box under your bed,' protested Sullivan, 'and you haven't been out of the cabin since the storm started. How could anyone have taken it?'

'How do I know?'

Here, thought Arthur, as he watched the two of them rocking wretchedly back and forth on their heels below him, here is a case for Sherlock Holmes! And he was just about to go and find him, when the great detective came through the door.

Not, though, without difficulty. He was being supported, to right and left, by Doctor Watson and Inspector Lestrade, and holding his left leg in what was obviously considerable agony! Arthur ran up to the distinguished trio.

'Mr Holmes!' he cried. 'What has happened? Did that red-bearded man attack you, did –'

Holmes allowed himself to be dropped into a chair. He stared blankly at Arthur.

'I have been bitten on my knee,' he said, 'by the Duchess of Cricklewood.'

'So there is still no sign of the red-bearded man?' inquired Arthur, as they sat in the saloon, a little later, while Sherlock Holmes, his knee bandaged into something resembling a white cauliflower by Doctor Watson, puffed his pipe and pondered.

'None,' replied Holmes. 'Of course, by now he has doubtless removed the beard and thrown it into the sea.'

'Oh, I doubt that, Holmes,' said Doctor Watson, putting away the stethoscope through which, for some unaccountable reason, he had been listening to the great detective's knee. 'I doubt that very much.'

'And why do you doubt that, Watson?'

'Elementary, my dear Holmes!' cried his friend, looking very pleased with himself. 'There has been not one single cry of "BEARD OVERBOARD!"'

Holmes looked at Arthur through the greeny-blue smoke.

'Has it ever occurred to you to wonder, Arthur,' he said, 'how Doctor Watson ever passed his medical exams?'

Arthur, of course, did not dream of replying to that; instead he said:

'At least we know that the red-bearded man wasn't after the Scarlet Horace, don't we?'

Holmes went a little pale.

'I very much doubt whether anyone would be silly enough to go after *that*,' he muttered. 'It is my opinion that Her Grace, The Duchess of Cricklewood, is descended from a long line of Alsatians.' His tall frame shuddered. 'I believe I shall carry to my grave the dreadful growl with which she sprang upon me as I entered her cabin and inquired as to the whereabouts of her wretched ruby! Had Watson and Lestrade not emptied the fire-bucket over her head, I am convinced she would have had my leg off.'

'And all the time,' said Arthur, 'some *real* criminal was making off with the priceless Gilbert and Sullivan manuscript.'

'*Some* real criminal?' snapped Sherlock Holmes. 'Who could it have been but our notorious red-bearded friend?'

'We don't know that for sure,' said Arthur.

Holmes set his jaw, and folded his arms, and looked away, out through the porthole towards the far blue horizon.

'*I* do,' he said. Then, as two familiar heads passed on the outside of the porthole, he removed his pipe to add, 'And here, Watson, unless I am very much mistaken, are our clients!'

'Sorry we're late,' said Gilbert, as he and Sullivan came into the saloon again, 'it took me a long time to get dressed. Couldn't do my buttons up, all fingers and thumbs, terribly nervous.' He sighed. 'All this has come as a terrible shock.'

'Quite, quite,' said Sherlock Holmes curtly. 'Now, there is just one more piece of information I need before settling down to consider your case, gentlemen, and that's this: was there anything else missing from your cabin, besides the manuscript?'

Gilbert nodded vigorously.

'Yes,' he answered, 'there was. A small tin trunk containing a number of props and costumes from the New York performance which we were taking back to England to use for the London opening.'

'Aha!' cried Holmes, springing to his feet, but wincing when he straightened his bitten knee. 'Just as I thought, Arthur! Would these props you mention include such items as beards?'

'Of course,' replied Sullivan. 'Could one have pirates without beards? Black beards, blond beards –'

'Red beards,' nodded Holmes, 'quite.'

Whereupon he whipped out from behind his chair the famous violin upon which he liked to play while pondering a particularly deep and tricky problem. Nobody else liked him to, though. As Sherlock Holmes began to saw away at *Three Blind Mice* (or, at least, at something roughly similar to *Three Blind Mice*), Arthur Seymour Sullivan looked just about as ill as it is possible for a professional musician to look.

And Arthur William Foskett crept quietly away.

But Arthur was not simply escaping from the great detective's terrible playing.

He wanted to do a little investigating of his own. Arthur did not quite know what it was that he was looking for; but he knew that there was no better way of starting an investigation than simply going about near the scene of the crime with your eyes and ears and your whole mind open.

First of all, naturally, he went to look in Gilbert's cabin. This was no longer locked, since everything of value had now gone. But there was nothing much to see: a bunk, a washbasin, a wardrobe, Gilbert's trouser-press and tooth-brush, and his breakfast tray on his bedside table.

Arthur looked at the breakfast tray for some time, thinking. He was still looking when the Chief Steward with the tattooed hands came in to collect it.

'Hallo!' said the Chief Steward cheerily. 'What are you doing here?'

'I was just having a look round,' said Arthur. He did not want anyone to know he was investigating. That would have been very rude to Sherlock Holmes, because this was, after all, supposed to be *his* case. 'I got a bit bored.'

'That's the way it is with ships,' said the Chief Steward, hefting the tray on to his broad shoulder. 'Just think how *I* must feel, day in, day out, back and forth across the bloomin' Atlantic all the time, you can go barmy. Yes,' he added, 'I'll be glad to pack it in, I don't mind saying.'

'You're giving up the sea?' said Arthur.

'Last trip,' said the Chief Steward happily, and strode out, crockery clinking.

I don't blame him for being happy, thought Arthur, who after a week had had more than enough of being stuck on the S.S. *Murgatroyd*. He stepped out on deck again.

And found himself face to face with the red-bearded man!

Who immediately turned on his heel, and ran off.

Now, Arthur was a very clever detective indeed. He knew that an ordinary detective – someone, say, like Inspector Lestrade – would probably have rushed after the red-bearded man yelling 'OY!' or 'STOP, THIEF!' or some such, but Arthur knew that that was the silliest possible action to

42

take. For it was essential not to let the red-bearded man know that anyone suspected him enough to follow him. So Arthur merely walked in the direction he had gone, though he did walk quite briskly, and sure enough, as he reached the corner of the deck-house and very, very carefully put an eye round it, he saw that the red-bearded man had slowed down, believing that nobody was chasing him.

After a few more steps, the man turned through a door into the deck-house. Arthur now ran quickly to this doorway, looked in, found himself at the top of a flight of stairs, and tiptoed down them. As he reached the bottom, he was just in time to see the red-bearded man disappear into a cabin.

Arthur paused only to note the number on the cabin door, then went back to the upper deck. With the calm seas and the crisp sunlight, more and more passengers were about, all looking cheerful enough after their grisly ordeal of the past few days, and strolling among them was, Arthur noticed, the Captain, who had clearly decided that he'd stayed away from them on the bridge long enough and ought at least to be civil, even though he reckoned passengers to be a bit of a nuisance.

Which is how he came to address Arthur.

'Good morning, Mr Foskett,' he said, smiling (it has to be said that the Captain preferred small boys to other sorts of passengers, because small boys, he'd noticed, tended to admire ship's captains, and the Captain had no objection at all to being admired).

'Good morning, Captain,' said Arthur. 'Thank you for handling the ship so very well during the storm.'

The Captain beamed!

'Not at all,' he cried, 'thank *you*! Yes, we've come through it jolly well, haven't we? Everyone seems to be bright and cheery again.'

'They do,' agreed Arthur. 'Especially the Bosun. I've never heard him in such good voice.'

It was true. The Bosun was strolling the upper deck, his fine polished peg striking the planking in time to the delightful shanty booming from his lips, his two eyes winking at the prettier ladies alternately, and his whole manner generally suggesting a remarkably happy man.

'Nor I,' said the Captain. 'He's truly marvellous at keeping up people's spirits, you know. Yes, I shall miss him, I'm afraid.'

'Miss him?' inquired Arthur.

'He's leaving at the end of the voyage,' replied the Captain. 'Giving up the sea. Can't imagine why.'

'It's probably because of his leg,' suggested Arthur.

'Leg? What about his leg?'

'Oh, it itches terribly, you know,' said Arthur, recalling the incident of the lifeboat. 'He has to keep taking it off.'

'Rubbish!' bellowed the Captain. 'Fiddlesticks! Why, I've sailed with him for thirty years, and he's never complained of it once. He's got one of the best peg-legs in the business, it was made for him by Queen Victoria's own carpenter, you won't see a better-built leg than that on Her Majesty's dining-table!'

Whereupon the Captain marched off to greet another passenger, leaving Arthur thinking that the affair of the Bosun's leg was getting more and more curious by the minute.

But he couldn't stand pondering all day; he had to report to Sherlock Holmes.

He found the detective struggling to play *God Save The Queen*. Arthur wondered briefly whether, if there had been anyone else in the saloon, they would have stood up while the anthem was played, but decided that they probably wouldn't have recognized it. As it was, the only person in there with the great detective was Doctor Watson, and as he had cotton wool in his

45

ears, he couldn't have been expected to stand either.

Holmes stopped playing when he saw Arthur, and Watson removed his ear-plugs.

'Ah, Watson,' said Sherlock Holmes, 'I believe Arthur has something important to tell us!'

'How on earth do you know that, Holmes?'

'Note,' said the great detective, 'that there is a little smudge of ink on Arthur's right hand. It was not there half an hour ago, when he went out for his walk. Now, why should Arthur bother to write anything down while out on a walk, unless it was something very important that he did not wish to forget?'

Even Arthur, who knew Holmes's methods, was impressed.

'Absolutely right first time, Mr Holmes!' he cried. 'I have seen the red-bearded man, and I have taken down the number of his cabin!'

Holmes leapt to his feet, casting aside his violin.

'Capital, Arthur!' he shouted. 'It is just the breakthrough I have been hoping for.'

'But nevertheless –' began Arthur.

'No buts!' roared Holmes. 'No neverthelesses! Let us hurry down and apprehend this appalling criminal immediately. Watson, call Lestrade!'

Arthur had no chance of making his point. Within seconds, all four of them were hurtling along the passage on the lower deck, towards the cabin of the red-bearded man!

'Keep back, Arthur!' muttered Holmes, as the three adults lined up in front of the cabin door. 'Watson, do you have your service revolver?'

Doctor Watson thrust his hand into his side-pocket confidently. And pulled out a banana.

Holmes glared at it.

'Interesting,' he hissed. 'I had not realized that the British Army was issuing service bananas!'

'Sorry, Holmes,' murmured Watson. 'You know how peckish I get. I'm afraid I've left my revolver in my cabin.'

'Then surprise must be our weapon!' said Holmes, and with a terrible cry he hurled himself bodily at the cabin door.

As it burst open, the red-bearded man jumped up from the bunk on which he had been lying, his eyes wide with horror. He opened his mouth, but no sound came out. Holmes grasped him by one arm, while Lestrade fastened on to the other.

'So,' shouted Sherlock Holmes, 'we have you, at last! Where is the manuscript, you blackguard?'

'Mr Holmes –'

'Be quiet, Arthur!' cried Holmes. 'Leave this to grown-ups! Watson, remove this villain's disguise!'

'No!' protested Arthur, but it was too late. Doctor Watson took hold of the bright red beard, and tugged.

'ow!' screamed its unfortunate owner.

'It won't come off, Holmes,' said Watson, confused.

'Of course it won't!' cried Arthur, who would normally never have dreamt of shouting an interruption; but this was an emergency. 'I've been trying to tell you that the beard is real!'

'Real?' exclaimed Holmes.

'Of course it's real!' moaned the red-bearded man.

'Yes,' said Arthur. 'I tried to point it out to you the very first time we saw him, Mr Holmes.'

'But look!' said Holmes angrily. 'The hair is black, the beard is red, so what do you make of *that*?'

'What I make of that,' said Arthur, quietly, 'is that the *hair* is false!'

'Good heavens,' murmured Holmes. 'Why didn't I think of that?'

Watson reached out, and the thick black wig came away in his hand, leaving a very bald red-bearded man glaring at them furiously.

'What,' he growled, now that he was recovering from the initial shock, 'is the meaning of this?'

'We're most awfully sorry,' said Arthur.

'No, we're not!' cried Lestrade.

'You will be,' muttered the red-bearded man.

'We *are* sorry,' said Arthur, firmly. 'You see, a valuable manuscript has been stolen, and everyone has been assuming, just because they thought your beard was false when it didn't match your hair, and because you kept running off and vanishing, that you were responsible. But I realized it wasn't you when it occurred to me that you wouldn't carry on wearing a false beard after you'd been spotted. The whole point of a disguise is that you get rid of it.'

'But why did he keep hiding, then?' asked the baffled Lestrade.

'Because,' said Arthur, 'his hair was false and it didn't match, and he was embarrassed in case the other passengers noticed.'

'He's right,' said the red-bearded man miserably. 'I usually have a nice red wig that matches my beard perfectly, but I took it to be cleaned especially for this voyage, and when I went to collect it, I found it had been dyed black by accident. It was too late to do anything about it.'

'But why wear it at all, then?' asked Holmes.

'It's freezing without it,' explained the red-bearded man. 'If I left it off in the middle of October after wearing it all these years, I'd catch my death of cold. Especially at sea.'

There was nothing left but to apologize to him. Fortunately, he was very understanding, as people usually are if you apologize sincerely for a genuine mistake.

'We appear,' said Holmes, when they were outside again, 'to be at a dead end.'

But Arthur said nothing.

Gilbert was gloomy. Sullivan was gloomy. But Sherlock Holmes was the gloomiest of all. He very rarely got things wrong, but when he did, he plunged himself into black misery.

'If only I could remember all my wonderful words,' moaned Gilbert.

'If only I could remember all my wonderful tunes,' groaned Sullivan.

'If only I'd taken a different boat,' muttered Holmes.

'If only they'd serve tea,' said Doctor Watson.

It was four p.m., and the saloon was filling with passengers hungry for cucumber sandwiches and Dundee cake after their bracing walks on deck, all chattering cheerily and paying no attention to the four gloomy gentlemen sitting in the middle of the room and staring at the floor. Who did not even notice that when Arthur joined them, he was smiling.

'Hallo,' said Arthur.

Holmes looked up, finally.

'I observe,' he said flatly, 'that you appear to be pleased with yourself. But for once in my life, I cannot deduce why.'

'I wonder,' said Arthur, 'if you would mind passing me your violin, Mr Holmes?'

'My – oh, very well.'

Watson reached for his cotton wool.

'I don't play too well,' said Arthur, tucking the instrument under his chin, 'but it's a pretty simple tune.'

And he played it. Just a few notes.

But the effect was astounding!

Arthur Sullivan leapt from his seat as if stung by a hornet!

'My tune!' he shouted, so loudly that at least a dozen passengers put down their teacups and one or two ladies looked as though they might faint again. 'My tune from *Patience*!'

But if the effect on the composer was remarkable, it was nothing to the effect upon the Chief Steward, who had come in to serve tea. As the few notes struck the air, the Chief Steward let out a great roar, and knocked over the sandwich trolley!

Egg-and-cress flew everywhere, fragments of tomato shot across the room, blobs of fish-paste slapped noisily against the ceiling!

'Curious!' observed Sherlock Holmes.

The Chief Steward got to his feet, but when he began handing round the teacups, his huge tattooed hands shook so much that the rattling made it almost impossible to speak! You could shout, though, which suited Sullivan very well.

'EXPLAIN YOURSELF, ARTHUR WILLIAM

FOSKETT!' he thundered, so that all the passengers who were writing to the company to complain began scribbling furiously on the backs of their menus. 'That tune is from the stolen manuscript. *It is known only to Gilbert and myself!'*

'Not quite,' murmured Sherlock Holmes. 'It is also known to Arthur. And,' he added, 'to me.'

Arthur nodded.

'The trouble was,' he said, 'that we weren't asking ourselves the two main questions. We were all too busy with the red beard business. And the first question *should* have been: who could have got into Mr Gilbert's cabin unnoticed?'

'Nobody,' retorted Gilbert. 'I was there all the time.'

'Yes,' said Arthur, 'you even had all your meals brought in, didn't you?'

'What of it?'

A huge figure bent over them.

'Cucumber sandwiches, gentlemen?' said the Chief Steward in a rather trembly voice, offering a tray.

Arthur looked up at him sternly.

'We were discussing,' he said, 'who might have entered Mr Gilbert's cabin unnoticed. Perhaps you could help?'

The Chief Steward took a deep breath, then sighed deeply.

'Nobody ever notices the steward,' he said, 'that is why I am giving up the sea.'

The listeners gasped! All, that is, except Arthur.

'Yes,' said Arthur, 'when I spotted the tray in Mr Gilbert's cabin, it all became clear. And then when you said that this was your last voyage, it became clearer still.' He turned to Gilbert. 'You see, he always came in with a tray, and he always came back to collect it from the floor beside your bed. And under the bed was the little tin box with the manuscript in it. It was the work of a second to pop the box on the tray, down there where you couldn't see, cover it with the tray-cloth, and carry it out.'

'Villain!' cried Sullivan, shaking his fist at the Chief Steward.

'Wait!' snapped Arthur. 'Never call people names before you've heard the whole story. Because we haven't yet come to the *second* question we forgot to ask. Which is: *why* on earth should anyone wish to steal the manuscript of an opera?'

'What?' cried Sullivan indignantly. 'The music is extremely valuable!'

'Nearly as valuable,' shouted Gilbert, 'as the words!'

'To whom?' asked Arthur, softly. 'I mean, nobody else could put the opera on without everyone knowing it was yours, and thus giving themselves away. The only possible point in stealing it would be *if the thief needed to know what was in it.*'

They thought about this for a while.

'All right,' said Gilbert to the Chief Steward, who was still hovering above them miserably, despite the fact that many of the other passengers were now growing extremely impatient for their tea, 'all right, I give up. Why *did* you want it?'

'Oh,' said Arthur, 'he didn't!'

'But someone else did,' murmured Sherlock Holmes, 'didn't they, Arthur?' And here Holmes's fine long intelligent face screwed up, as he dug down into his remarkable memory, and he sang a snatch of song to the tune which Arthur had played.

Gilbert went white!

'My words!' he cried. 'Where on earth did you hear them?'

'In a lifeboat,' said Sherlock Holmes.

'Of course,' said Arthur, 'he doesn't sing them nearly as well as the Bosun does.'

Whereupon Arthur clapped his hands, and into the saloon burst a very impressive figure indeed! He wore a magnificent blue uniform with golden epaulettes and a crimson sash, and a splendid silver helmet with a great purple plume in it, and one shimmering black riding boot on the leg that wasn't wooden!

'Our props!' cried Gilbert and Sullivan together. 'Our clothes!'

'Precisely!' said Arthur. And while the amazed passengers stared, the Bosun expanded his enormous bemedalled chest, and sang:

'When I first put this uniform on,
I said as I looked in the glass:
It's one to a million that any civilian
My figure and form could surpass.'

Which, as you know, was the song that Holmes
and Arthur had heard him singing in the lifeboat;
but now he sang it full-bloodedly and beautifully,
and he did not stop there. He sang four more songs
from the vanished manuscript of *Patience*, and
when he at last had finished, not only were the
passengers stamping and cheering and tearing up
all their letters of complaint to the company, but
Gilbert and Sullivan were beaming and applaud-
ing, too!

The Bosun, after taking several bows, stumped
over to their table and gave a final, very low,
bow.

'Gentlemen,' he said humbly, 'I cannot apologize enough. But there was no other way.'

'To do what?' cried Sullivan.

The Bosun turned to Arthur.

'Would you explain?' he said. 'You put things so
well.'

'The Bosun,' said Arthur, 'is leaving the sea
after this voyage, just like his best friend, the Chief
Steward. But he is not leaving because his leg
itches. That was just a little fib I shall come to later,
because it was a fib that put me on to him, after the
Captain had told me the leg never itched at all. No,

the Bosun is leaving because he wants to become a singer.'

'Aha!' exclaimed Holmes. 'It begins to fit! Go on, Arthur.'

'He has been training his voice for years,' continued Arthur, 'and all the time he was wondering how he could bring himself to the attention of the musical world. And then, miracle of miracles, he learned that Mr Gilbert and Mr Sullivan were travelling home on the S.S. *Murgatroyd*, bringing with them the manuscript of their new opera! Just suppose, he said to himself – and he'd be the first to admit it was a bit wicked – just suppose I borrowed that manuscript, and learned it by heart, hidden in a lifeboat, and sang it for them, might they not recognize my talent, possibly even give me a part in *Patience* when it opened?'

'But couldn't he –' began Sullivan.

'I think I know what you're going to say, sir,' said the Bosun. 'Why couldn't I come along and audition for *Patience* in the normal way? But ask yourself this – would you even bother to audition an ordinary sailorman? I wouldn't have got within a mile of the theatre.'

'He's right, you know,' said Gilbert. 'I think we can count ourselves jolly lucky he hit on his idea, Sullivan.'

'And *he* can count himself jolly lucky,' said Sullivan, 'that he had a good and brave friend like the Chief Steward who was ready to pinch *Patience* for him.'

'Lucky?' cried the Bosun. 'You mean you'll give me a chance?'

'Give you a part, is what we mean,' beamed Sullivan. 'I thought you sang the melodies superbly!'

'Not,' said Gilbert, 'that that's particularly important. The main thing is, I could understand every wonderful word!'

'Hurrah!' cried the Chief Steward.

'There would seem,' said Sherlock Holmes, 'to be just one mystery left to clear up. Which is – where is the precious manuscript now?'

Everyone looked at Arthur.

'We come,' said Arthur, as the Bosun nodded encouragingly, 'to the question of the fib. If the Bosun wasn't suffering from itchiness, Mr Holmes, why did he take his leg off in the lifeboat?'

Holmes nodded sagely.

'I thought as much,' he said.

But, of course, unlike Arthur, he had only *just* thought as much!

And, as all the passengers watched in amazement, the Bosun unstrapped his leg once more, and passed it across to Arthur, with a broad smile.

'I think you ought to do the honours, Arthur,' he said.

So Arthur took the gleaming mahogany leg in both hands, and turned it, and it unscrewed at the middle, revealing, safe and sound, the rolled-up manuscript of *Patience*!

Sherlock Holmes could restrain himself no longer. Slapping Arthur on the shoulder, he cried:

'Capital! Capital!'

Doctor Watson, of course, cried, 'Amazing!'

And Arthur, of course, murmured:

'Elementary.'

Heard about the Puffin Club?

... it's a way of finding out more about Puffin books and authors, of winning prizes (in competitions), sharing jokes, a secret code, and perhaps seeing your name in print! When you join you get a copy of our magazine, *Puffin Post*, sent to you four times a year, a badge and a membership book.

For details of subscription and an application form, send a stamped addressed envelope to:

The Puffin Club Dept A
Penguin Books Limited
Bath Road
Harmondsworth
Middlesex UB7 0DA

and if you live in Australia, please write to:

The Australian Puffin Club
Penguin Books Australia Limited
P.O. Box 257
Ringwood
Victoria 3134